Hailey Twitch
and the Wedding Glitch

Hailey Twitch by Lauren Barnholdt

Hailey Twitch Is Not a Snitch

Hailey Twitch and the Great Teacher Switch

Hailey Twitch and the Campground Itch

Hailey Twitch

and the Wedding Glitch

Lauren Barnholdt

Pictures by Suzanne Beaky

sourcebooks
jabberwocky

Published by Sourcebooks Jabberwocky, an imprint of Sourcebooks, Inc.
P.O. Box 4410, Naperville, Illinois 60567-4410
(630) 961-3900
Fax: (630) 961-2168
www.jabberwockykids.com

Library of Congress Cataloging-in-Publication data is on file with the publisher.

Source of Production: Webcom, Toronto, Ontario, Canada
Date of Production: September 2011
Run Number: 16052

Printed and bound in Canada.
WC 10 9 8 7 6 5 4 3 2 1

For Aaron, always

Contents

Chapter One

Wonderful News

Something very wonderful is happening right at this very moment. And that wonderful thing is called being a flower girl! Yay! The flower girl is the most important part in a wedding. That is because she is in charge of dropping beautiful rose petals onto the ground right in front of the bride.

The bride is my cousin, Genevieve. She is getting married in one week.

That means that in seven whole days I get to wear a fab, fab, fabulous princess dress. Because that is what flower girls do. In fact, that is where I am right now. At the fabulous princess dress shop. It is called BRIDES AND MORE. And it is only for dresses for weddings. For brides. And flower girls.

"I want this one!" I yell. I am run, run, running right into the store and right up to a very beautiful white long dress with lace all on it.

"Hailey," my mom says. "That is a dress for a bride."

"Or a flower girl," I say.

"A bride," she says.

"Or a flower girl," I tell her.

"No," my mom says.

"Why not?" I look around for someone who works in that store. I see a lady over in the corner. She is wearing a name tag. And she has very frizzy brown hair. "Excuse me, lady!" I yell. "We need some help with this dress right over here. We need to wrap one up for a flower girl."

That lady does not look too happy at all about the yelling. But she comes over anyway.

"Can I help you?" she asks. Then she points over to a sign that is hanging on the wall. I sound out the words. PLEASE WATCH CHILDREN IN THE STORE, it says.

I am a child. Because I am seven years old. But I do not need to be watched. On account of me being a flower girl.

"That sign is not very nice," I tell that lady. "I am going to be a very beautiful flower girl in my cousin Genevieve's wedding." I do a curtsy so she can tell just how beautiful it will be. "And I would like you to wrap up this dress, please."

"That is a bride's dress," the lady says. She is getting a little bit of a mean voice. Kind of like the voice my neighbor Mr. Frisk uses when I am bothering him.

"No, it isn't," I say. "It is not just for brides. Flower girls can wear it, too." I am about to have a good tantrum right in this store. I can feel it already starting right up inside of me.

"Hailey," my mom says. Then she points over toward the door. "Look who it is! It's your cousin Angela!"

I turn around to look. And there is Cousin Angela. She is walking right into the store of Brides and More. She is with Aunt Denise.

Aunt Denise is Angela's mom. And she is my mom's sister. It is all a very confusing family tree.

"What are those two doing here?" I ask. "Is Aunt Denise getting married, too?"

"No," my mom says. "Aunt Denise is already married to Uncle Adam. You know that."

"Then why are they coming to a bride shop, please? Are they going to take pictures of me in my princess dress?" That would be very fun. I will pose and pose and pose. And then I will put those pictures in beautiful frames all over the house. I will even autograph them with my nickname "Hails."

"Well," my mom says. She is getting a very nervous look on her face. It is the look she gets right when she is about to tell me something terrible. "Cousin Angela is going to be a flower girl, too. Isn't that wonderful?"

I get a very dark face on. That is not wonderful

5

news. That is very bad and horrible news. And I am already at my limit for bad news.

That is because I am already dealing with some bad news about my magic sprite Maybelle. And that is that she might have to go back to living in her magic castle and leave the Twitch house for good.

Mr. Tuttle, who is in charge of the Department of Magic, said so. He said he will be coming back very soon to take Maybelle away.

This is making me very sad.

It is making Maybelle very sad, too. Even though she does not look so sad right now. Right now she is curled up in a shoe in this store having a nap.

"That is not such wonderful news about Cousin Angela," I tell my mom. "There is only supposed to be one flower girl." And that one flower girl should be me. But I do not say that last part.

"Hello, Aunt Denise and Cousin Angela!" my mom is saying.

Cousin Angela is wearing very dirty overalls. She is five. And she picks her nose. I have seen her do it lots and lots of times. "Hailey, say hello," my mom says.

"Hello."

"Now, girls, you are going to have to pick out the same dress," Aunt Denise says. I am worried about this for one minute. But then I remember that I am seven. And Cousin Angela is only five. So I am the boss of her for definite.

"Why don't I show you some flower girl dresses that we just got in," the saleslady says. She takes my mom and Aunt Denise over to some dresses. Some dresses that look like they were made for babies.

"Cousin Angela, wouldn't you like to wear this wonderful, beautiful, perfect dress?" I show her that wonderful bride dress that I picked right out. It is very sparkly. "It has jewels all on it," I say. "It is for princesses."

"No," Cousin Angela says. "That dress is ugly."

"It is not," I say. I am feeling very upset in my heart about all of this. That dress is very beautiful and very perfect, and I want it.

"Yes. It. Is," Angela says. Then she puts her finger right in her nose. That is very disgusting.

"That," I say, "is very disgusting. Nose picking is what disgusting babies do."

Angela makes her eyes look very small in her head. And then she stomps right down on my foot very hard.

"Ow!" I scream, jumping up and down like a maniac. "Ow, ow, ow!"

"Wow," Maybelle says. She is waking up from her nap. On account of all the yelling, I think.

"Cousin Angela is not very well behaved."

My mom and Aunt Denise are looking around to see what all this big fuss is about.

"Hailey," my mom says. "Why are you screaming like that?"

"I am screaming like that because Cousin Angela stomped right on my foot." I hop, hop, hop right over to

her on one foot only. Even though that foot is not really even hurting anymore.

"No, I did not," Angela says. "Hailey is being a bad liar." And then that little five-year-old baby starts crying. Right in the store. That is called having a meltdown in public.

"Yes, you did," I say. I shake, shake, shake my finger right at her. "You stepped right on it and crushed my toes. And so now you need to have a punishment."

Aunt Denise picks Cousin Angela up into her arms. Cousin Angela is too old to be getting picked up, if you ask me. Then Aunt Denise says, "Girls, please. No fighting. Let's go look at the flower girl dresses that are over here."

"Come on, Hailey," my mom says. She walks to the back of the store. Aunt Denise follows her right away. And Cousin Angela sticks her tongue out at me! Right when no one can see.

"That girl is a brat," Maybelle says.

"Yes," I say, very sad. "She is. And me and her have got to be flower girl twins."

It is enough to make a girl very upset.

Chapter Two

- - - - - - - - - - - - - - - - - - - -

A Sprite with Problems

We have to leave that store without even getting a dress! And that is because Cousin Angela was in a very cranky mood. She was being very loud in that store. I read that sign right out loud to Aunt Denise about watching your children. But she just ignored me. Which is very rude if you want to know the truth.

The one good thing is that we stop at the drive-through on the way home. I love stopping at the drive-through! We used to do it a lot more. But now we are only eating healthy dinners and snacks. So it is not allowed.

I lean over in the car and say the order

right into the microphone. I say, "Please, can I have some French fries and one order of chicken nuggets?"

Then the man says, "What did you say?"

So I say it again. Only this time much more loud.

"Who has been eating these fries?" my big sister Kaitlyn says when we get home. She is looking in the bag. And seeing all the missing fries.

I sit down at the kitchen table. And then I quick try and change the subject. Maybe because I was the one eating those fries. It was a very hungry drive home. "Cousin Angela stomped right down on my foot," I tell Kaitlyn. I hold my foot up. "Because we cannot agree on the same dress. I might have a broken toe and need a cast around it."

"Ew, Hailey," Kaitlyn says. "Get your sneakers off the table."

She is unpacking all the bags and putting those very delicious nuggets right in front of me. Then she takes out the little tub of honey mustard. She takes the top off it and sets it down.

"Thank you for opening my honey mustard, Kaitlyn. You are a very good sister."

"You're welcome, Hailey."

"I want to try one of those fries," Maybelle says. She sits down on the table and starts munching on one of them.

"Kaitlyn," I say. "What do you think about Cousin Genevieve's wedding, please?"

"Weddings are boring." Kaitlyn takes a big bite of her ooey, gooey cheeseburger.

"They are not boring," I say. "Not when you are getting to be a flower girl." I reach out and give Kaitlyn a little pat on her hand. Kaitlyn is very jealous, probably. Because she is fourteen years old. And fourteen is too old to be a flower girl. "It is okay to be jealous. It happens to the best of us."

Kaitlyn rolls her eyes and takes one of my fries. She almost smacks Maybelle right in the head with it.

"So, Kaitlyn," I say. "What am I going to do about this whole problem?"

"What whole problem?" She has her cell phone out. She is texting away on it. Probably to her friend Maya Greenbert. All about boys, boys, boys.

"The whole problem with this dress and Cousin Angela!"

"I do not know." Kaitlyn is very good with helping with problems. But sometimes she does not want to help. "But there might not even be a wedding."

"What do you mean?" I am gasping at this horrible news.

"You think they can really plan a whole wedding in one week? That is crazy."

"One week is enough time. One week is forever. It is seven whole days."

"They don't even have a band picked out," Kaitlyn says. "How can they have a wedding without music?"

"It will all work out," I tell her. That is what my dad tells me whenever I am having a problem. Usually my problem is about Natalie Brice, the meanest girl in room four, Miss Stephanie's second grade.

When I am finished with my dinner, I go upstairs.

"Maybelle," I say. "Help me with my problem, please."

"Your problem?" Maybelle asks. "What about my problem?" She is flying all around my room.

"You do not have any problems," I grumble. "You are just a magic sprite." Magic sprites do not even have to worry about being flower girls. They do not have to worry about stupid babies named Cousin Angela. They do not have to worry about broken toes that probably need a big cast on them. And they do not have to worry about finding music for that wedding.

"I am very much in trouble with Mr. Tuttle!" Maybelle says. "Maybe you forgot all about that big disaster."

"I did not forget," I say. "But me and you came up with a very good plan about that."

Mr. Tuttle is in charge of the Department of Magic. And he told Maybelle that if she did very good magic, then he would give her magic back to her forever! And so Maybelle did very good at her magic. But then Mr. Tuttle told her that now she is going to have to go back to living in the magic castle forever and ever and ever.

Maybelle does not want to go back to that castle. She wants to live here, in the Twitch house. With me. Like two friends forever!

So I came up with a very brilliant plan. And that plan is that Maybelle is going to be very bad at her magic again. One big mess of a magic sprite. And then Mr. Tuttle will think she needs some more work. And so she will get to stay here! It is very perfect.

"I do not think that plan is going to work," Maybelle says. She is standing in front of my mirror, and she is looking at herself and those sparkly wings of hers.

"Maybelle," I tell her, doing a big sigh. "I am very good at brilliant plans." This is a little bit of a fib. Some of my plans do not always work out so well. Like the time I decided to pick some apples in my neighbor Mr. Frisk's backyard. It turned out those apples were not ready to be picked. Or the time I decided to draw a big mustache on my friend Addie Jokobeck's face with a black marker. That is against the rules of room four.

"Just be very bad at your magic," I tell Maybelle. "And you will not have to go back to that castle." I am looking all around in my drawer to find a very good gymnastics suit. Gymnastics suits are also called bodysuits or

18

leotards. I have lots of them. A blue one. A green one. A red one. And a black one. That is because I am always doing gymnastics. Also because they were on sale one day.

But my favorite gymnastics suit is my sparkly white bathing suit. It is not really a gymnastics suit. But it is sparkly. And it has a skirt on it.

"I am going to put on my gymnastics suit now," I tell Maybelle. "And then I am going to do some handstands against my bedroom wall." This is technically supposed to be not allowed. But I have had a very rough day.

But before I can even put that perfect gymnastics suit on, Maybelle pulls out her wand. And she points it right at the gymnastics suit. And then that gymnastics suit turns green! And all the sparkles are gone, and the skirt disappears right away!

"Maybelle!" I yell. "What did you do to this gymnastics suit?"

"I am being bad at my magic," she whispers. "So Mr. Tuttle will think I lost it."

"You should not have wrecked this gymnastics suit!" I tell her. "This is my most very favorite one. Make it go back to being sparkly right this instant."

"No, thank you," Maybelle says. And then she goes away.

I have decided to give Maybelle the silent treatment. The silent treatment is when you do not talk to someone because they have been very, very bad. My mom gives my dad the silent treatment when he forgets to tie up the garbage can and the neighbors' dogs get into it and spread it all over our lawn and my mom has to clean it up before work.

I give Maybelle the silent treatment all night.

I am still giving it to her the next morning at school, even. I am giving it to her all through the Pledge of Allegiance. And all through printing time. And all through morning snack.

It is supposed to make Maybelle mad, mad, mad. But she does not even care.

I decide it is more fun to think about being a flower girl.

"Hey, Russ," I say to my friend Russ Robertson when we are walking down the hall to music class. "Did you hear that wonderful news about how I am going to be a flower girl?"

"Hailey," Addie Jokobeck whispers. "We are not supposed to be talking in line."

This is a true fact. But we are at the back of the line. And Miss Stephanie is in the front. So as long as I am quiet as a mouse, she will not hear me. I do not like being at the back of the line. I like to be line leader. But this week line leader is Antonio Fuerte. And this week I am in charge of watering the plants on the windowsill.

"Hey, Russ," I whisper, so that Addie Jokobeck cannot hear. "Did you hear about me being a flower girl?"

"No," Russ says. And then he faces right forward.

"Wow," Maybelle says. "Russ does not even care."

I give her a mean look. Then I say, "Yup, I am going to be a flower girl with a beautiful white bride dress and a beautiful sparkly tiara made of real diamonds that cost a hundred dollars."

"Flower girl dresses cannot be white bride dresses," Natalie Brice says. Natalie is the meanest girl in room four. She has curly hair and roller-skate shoes. She is a very big show-off. And she thinks she is the boss of me.

"Yes, they can, Natalie," I tell her.

"No, they cannot."

"How do you even know about flower girl dresses, Natalie Brice?"

"Because," she says. "I have been a flower girl five whole different times. When I was a baby, like four years old."

But before I can even say anything back, we are at the music room.

Music is a very fun class. It is even more fun when we get to play instruments. These are all the instruments to choose from: triangle, bongo drums, harmonica, pipe. The instruments are in a big basket in the middle of the room.

Our music teacher, Mr. Green, lets us pick out whatever instrument we want!

And so we all go running up to the basket. I am push, push, pushing so I can get those bongo drums. Bongo drums are the best instrument to have. You can pound on them very hard. And you can be the loudest one of all of the instruments.

There is one more reason those bongo drums are the best to have. And that is because when we are done with our instrument unit, we are going to get to keep those instruments to bring home! So if you have the bongo drums, you might get to keep them all for your own self.

But I do not end up with the bongo drums. Instead I end up with the very worst instrument. And that is the instrument of the harmonica.

"Natalie Brice!" I yell. "Pushing is not allowed!"

"I was not pushing," she says. She gives a little sniff with her nose. And then she pounds right on those bongo drums with the drumstick.

"Mr. Green!" I say. I wave my hand in the air all around. "Mr. Green! Natalie Brice is pushing, and she stepped right on my toe!"

"What is going on over here, girls?" Mr. Green asks.

"Natalie pushed me and stepped on my toe. It's broken."

"Your toe is broken?" Mr. Green asks. He is looking very confused on his face.

Natalie does a big sigh. "Oh, Hailey Twitch," she says. "You have a very big imagination." Natalie Brice is always trying to use big words and pretend she is a grown-up.

"My toe got broken yesterday at a bride store," I explain to Mr. Green. "I might need to get a cast on it. And then Natalie stepped on it while she was pushing to get those bongo drums." I hop up and down. "Ow, my bad toe, ow!"

I am hoping Mr. Green is going to tell Natalie to hand those drums right over to me. But he does not. All he does is say, "I'm sure your toe will feel better soon, Hailey. Now, everyone, please line up so we can have a parade."

I am still mad. But I do get cheered up a little by that parade. It is only a parade around the classroom. But it is very loud. Things that are that loud make me very hap, hap, happy.

I get in line between Addie Jokobeck and Russ Robertson.

Then I whisper to Maybelle, "Maybelle, please make Natalie Brice's drums to be not that loud. Make them all very quiet as a mouse so that no one hears them." This is one of the good things about having a wonderful magic sprite. You can make her use her magic to do things you want.

But when our parade starts, something very horrible happens. And that is that my harmonica is broken! It does not even make one noise. I am blowing, blowing, blowing into it hard, hard, hard. Even harder than one time when I had to blow up seven whole red balloons for my birthday party.

"Stop the parade!" I yell. "Stop this parade right this minute! Hailey Twitch's harmonica is broken!" But no one can hear me. Everyone just keeps march, march, marching. They are not even paying one bit of attention to me. I look around for Maybelle.

She is over sitting on the top of Natalie Brice's bongo drums. I have a bad feeling in my stomach. And that bad feeling has to do with Maybelle making my harmonica quiet.

Chapter Three

Sparkly Shoes

"Maybelle," I say to her when we are home. I am outside throwing a ball against the garage and catching it. *Bang. Bang. Bang.* It is very fun. "What you did in music class was very naughty."

"I had to do it," she says. "That is me being bad at my magic."

I throw the ball against the house again. *Slam!*

"No, that is you making Natalie Brice have very loud bongo drums like I wanted. And then you made my harmonica quiet. That is not very fun or funny, Maybelle."

Then I start to get a very good idea. The music for the wedding! If I am allowed to keep those bongo drums, then I can make the music. I will save the day with those drums!

I am getting very excited about this plan. Then I hear a very familiar sound. A very familiar drum sound. A very familiar drum sound that sounds just like those bongo drums. I look down to where Maybelle is sitting on a rock. She somehow has some tiny bongo drums. And tiny drumsticks, too, even.

"Maybelle," I say, "where did you get those?"

"Out of the play school-house in the corner of room one."

"Room one is kindergarten," I say. "You cannot just go around stealing things from kindergarten."

"I am just borrowing

it. For maybe a few days." She starts to play those wonderful drums. "It is a very fun instrument."

"I know," I say. I am in a very grumpy mood from all of this.

Maybelle is really having fun with those drums. She is on the grass now and pretending she is having a big parade. She is taking very big steps, up, down, up, down, up, down.

"Be in my parade, Hailey!" she yells.

"No, thank you," I tell her. "I am too mad at you."

But that parade does look very fun. So I decide that maybe I will be in it after all. So I go and get behind Maybelle. And we are marching all over the lawn. I do not have an instrument. Not even that dumb harmonica. But I pretend I have some very big cymbals. And I am crashing them. *Crash! Crash! Crash!*

We are going around and around and around

the yard. I am waving to the imaginary crowd. But then something bad happens.

Maybelle is taking such big steps that she falls right into a big mud puddle! And a big thing of ooey, gooey, disgusting sticky brown mud goes flying up in the air and splatters all over me.

"Uh-oh," I say. I look down at my shirt. I do not care about mud too much. But my mom does care about it. She does not like it when I get all dirty. I am just deciding that it is time to go upstairs and maybe have a quick change before my mom can see.

But then my mom comes right outside. "Hailey!" she says. "Why are you all dirty? We are supposed to be going to another dress shop! Now get upstairs and change right now, young lady!"

- -

My mom is very mad. On account of all that mud.

She is very quiet and giving me the silent treatment all the way to the dress shop. This dress shop is different than the one from yesterday.

And it does not have the dress I wanted. But it does have sparkly shoes! Beautiful glittery sparkly shoes that are glimmery and gorgeous.

"These are the shoes for me!" I yell. I take them right off the shelf and put them right on my feet. "How do I look?" I am shuf, shuf, shuffling all around the store. It is very fun. The saleslady gives me a big smile. She is a nice one. There are no signs on the walls here about keeping your children tied up and quiet.

But then something not that fun happens. And that is Cousin Angela coming into the store. "Those shoes are mine!" she screams very loud at the top of her lungs.

"No, they are not," I say. "These are my

shoes. You will have to get your own pair." I am trying to get away from her. But the shoes are too big. And so I trip right onto the floor. And those shoes go flying. And Angela picks them up and puts them right on her own feet.

"Mom!" I scream. "Angela took my shoes!"

That saleslady comes right over. She is not

smiling so much anymore. She tells us that it is time for us to leave because we are making a big scene. I guess they do not like children in this store either. My mom and Aunt Denise are not very happy. Not even one little bit.

"Please," I tell the saleslady. "I will be good. I promise. We are going to spend a lot of money in this store."

I have a feeling that those glitter shoes are going to be very a lot of money. Maybe even more than one hundred dollars.

The saleswoman is putting her lips together very tight.

"You're pretty," Angela says to her.

"Well, aren't you just so cute?" the saleslady says. "I have a beautiful blue flower girl dress that would just look perfect on you."

"What about me?" I ask. "Do you have any good pink dresses that would look good on me, Hailey Twitch? Or maybe a white bride dress?"

"Who are you?" the saleslady asks me. She is looking down at Angela and giving her a nice big smile. "Are you this adorable little girl's sister?"

"No," I say. "I am the flower girl."

"I AM THE FLOWER GIRL!" Angela yells.

"There cannot be two flower girls," the saleslady says.

I take a big sigh. This is going to be a long day.

- -

Finally we have picked out the dress! The most beautiful perfect blue dress in the whole wide world. My mom and Aunt Denise think I look very beautiful in it. And I have not even said the best part. And that best part is that I am going to get to wear a crown. A crown of flowers! Blue and white ones that are very fancy. A crown of real flowers is very much better than a jewel crown.

I am so happy that I am skip, skip, skipping into school the next day.

"Guess what, Addie Jokobeck?" I ask her. "I am going to have a beautiful blue dress and a crown full of flowers to wear when I am a flower girl."

"Wow," Addie Jokobeck says. Her mouth goes right into the shape of an O. "I wish I was going to be a flower girl."

"I will see if my mom will let me bring in my crown of flowers, and I will let you wear it," I say. I am crossing my fingers behind my back when I am saying this. And that is because I am not going to really ask my mom. She would never give me a permission for that. But I am going to bring it in anyway.

"When I was a flower girl, I got to wear a sparkly tiara," Natalie Brice says. "It had diamonds. Real ones. And my dress was a lot fancier than yours."

"That is a big lie, Natalie," I say. "You did not have real diamonds on your crown. And you are just jealous of my blue dress."

"I think *you* are a big liar," Natalie says. "You are probably not even going to be a flower girl. You are always lying."

There is only one thing to do. And that is to wear my flower girl dress to school.

on the sink. It is blue nail polish. And it is Kaitlyn's. I am too young to have nail polish.

But Cousin Angela does not know that. So I say, "That nail polish is mine."

"You are allowed to wear nail polish?" Cousin Angela asks. She has lots of soap, soap, soapy suds on her hands.

"Of course."

"No, you are not," Maybelle says. "That is Kaitlyn's nail polish." Maybelle is washing her hands, too.

I give her a look to be quiet. Even though Cousin Angela cannot hear her. It is not any of Maybelle's business about that nail polish. It is nobody's business but my own self's.

"My mommy says nail polish is only for big girls," Cousin Angela says.

Chapter Four

A Big Blue Mess

"Hailey," Maybelle says, "You cannot be wearing your dress to school. That is not allowed."

"It is going to be fine," I tell her. It is later that night. Me and Maybelle are in the kitchen. And we are setting the table. That is because Cousin Angela and Aunt Denise are coming over. They are bringing our dresses. And we are going to try them on. And then tomorrow, I will wear mine to school! And I will show that Natalie Brice that I am not a liar. It is a completely wonderful plan.

"What if you get that dress dirty?" Maybelle asks.

"I do not get dirty."

"You fell in a big mud puddle the other day."

"Maybelle! That is not polite." I am putting all the spoons down on the table. That is because my mom is making a delicious broccoli soup for an appetizer. Broccoli is not good. But it is good in soup. I drop Cousin Angela's spoon right on the floor. Whoops.

I pick it up.

"You better get her another one," Maybelle says.

"Looks clean to me." I put it back down next to her plate.

When Cousin Angela and Aunt Denise get over, they have Cousin Genevieve with them. She is the bride. And so she wants to see us in our dresses.

"Now, Maybelle," I whisper

to her. "Do not be causing any mischief with the dresses."

"I will if I want," Maybelle says. Then she whispers, "I am trying to be bad at magic, remember?"

I have a weird feeling about this right in my stomach. But I cannot think about it too long.

And that is because those wonderful dresses are coming right out of their dress bags.

"I will try mine on first!" I say. I go rushing right at it and try to make a grab for that dress.

"Hailey!" Cousin Genevieve yells, pulling it away. "You have to wash your hands first. We cannot get this dress dirty."

I do a big sigh. Washing your hands is for babies. My hands are clean as a whistle. But me and Cousin Angela go in the bathroom to wash up.

"Whose nail polish is that?" Cousin Angela asks. She is looking at the bottle that is sitting

"Well, I am a big girl." I dry my hands off on a purple towel. "I am seven years old." I pick up the nail polish and take the top off. Then I paint my one pinkie nail blue. "See?" I say. "It is mine."

I put the cap back on. "Now come on. We have to try our dresses on."

"BLUE NAILS FOR ME, TOO!" Cousin Angela yells.

"No," I tell her. "Blue nails are for big girls only."

"ANGELA IS A BIG GIRL!" Cousin Angela screams. And then she picks up that bottle of nail polish. I grab it. And I try to pull it out of her hands. But she pulls it back very hard.

"Let go right this instant," I tell her. "I am seven, and you are five, and that means I am the boss of you." But Cousin Angela does not listen. She pulls on it harder.

And then that bottle of nail polish goes flying into the air. It is spinning around and around and around, and I reach up and try to catch it. But I miss. I knock right into it with my hand. Nail polish goes spilling and splattering all over. Blue is splattering on the walls and all over us.

Cousin Angela looks at me. She has a speckle of blue nail polish right on the tip of her nose. "You made a mess," she says. "Now you are going to be in big trouble, mister."

"I did not make a mess," I say. "You did."

"No, you!"

"No!"

"You, you, you!" Then Cousin Angela moves over to the sink. There is a pool of blue nail polish right in there. She dips her fingers in that blue. And then she smears them right on her cheek. "Face paint!" she says. "HAHAHAHAHAHA."

Wow. She is laughing a lot about that face paint. She thinks it is the most hilarious thing ever invented.

"Maybelle," I whisper. "Please, please, please use your magic to clean this place up. If you do, I will be your best friend."

"Your best friend is Addie Jokobeck," Maybelle says. She is dipping her nails into that polish, too.

"But you will be my new one," I say. "If you clean it up. And we can do all the fun things that best friends forever do!"

Maybelle thinks about it. Then she pulls her wand out. She points it at that nail polish bottle. And then it is flying back up into the air and even more nail polish is coming out.

"Ahhh!" Cousin Angela screams.

"Ahhh!" I scream.

It is all over. Like a big rainstorm of blue sticky nail polish.

My mom and Aunt Denise and Cousin Genevieve come running into the bathroom.

"Girls!" my mom says. "What is all this

yelling about?" Then she sees that very big mess. "Hailey," she says. "Please go to your room."

- -

We cannot try on the dresses. And dinner with the broccoli soup is even canceled. That is because Cousin Angela and I are two big messes covered in blue nail polish. We both need to have baths immediately.

"Why did you do that, Maybelle?" I ask when I am in my bath. I am covered all up in bubbly bubbles. I have a very scratchy sponge. I am supposed to be scrub, scrub, scrubbing all up.

"You know why," Maybelle whispers. "I am trying to be bad at magic so that Mr. Tuttle will not make me go back to the castle."

"Yes, but you could have been bad at magic without making a big mess." This nail polish is not very good at coming off of skin. It is stuck right on my arms no matter how hard I scrub.

"Or you could have made that big mess go on Cousin Angela only."

"Hailey!" my mom calls. "Did you get all that nail polish off yet?"

"I am getting there!" I say. There is still some blue on my legs. And on my arms. But I am wearing long sleeves and long pants for pajamas so no one will have to know. It will be like my own little secret.

- -

The next morning I wake up for school very, very early. It is so exciting that I can hardly wait. And that is because I am going to be wearing that flower girl dress right to school!

But first it is time for breakfast.

"Hello," I say when I get downstairs. "Good morning, Kaitlyn!" I am wearing jeans. And a gray T-shirt with a big smiley face on the front. That is a trick. So that no one will think I am wearing my dress to school. Because Maybelle is right about that. It is not allowed.

"What are you up to?" Kaitlyn asks me. She is sitting right at the table eating a bowl of oatmeal.

"I am not up to anything," I tell her. I am trying to look very innocent on my face. I go to get my cereal bowl out of the cupboard.

"Yes, you are," she says. "You are not wearing anything sparkly. And you are being very nice to me. You are up to something. "

"I am being nice to you," I say, "because I am very sorry that I spilled your blue nail polish all over."

"You spilled it all over?" Kaitlyn says. "That was a brand-new bottle of nail polish!"

"Yes, well, Cousin Angela was pretending to be a big girl. And she knocked it all over." I push the box of Apple O's across the table to her. "Would you like some cereal, Kaitlyn? I will pour it for you."

"Mom!" Kaitlyn yells. "Mom!"

My mom comes running into the kitchen. She is wearing some very fancy work clothes of black pants and black high-heeled shoes. "Wowza," I say. "You look like a knockout."

"Thank you," she says. She pours some Apple O's into my bowl.

"Mom, Hailey spilled my nail polish all over, and I just bought that nail polish with my babysitting money!" Kaitlyn says. Kaitlyn thinks she is so smart because she has a babysitting job.

"Everyone just stay calm," I say. "It is just some nail polish. It is not the end of the world." Some people have real problems. Like getting music at the wedding. And stopping their sprite from having to go back to the castle.

I take a big spoonful of Apple O's. One falls off my spoon and onto the table. Maybelle picks it up and starts to eat it right up. Apple O's are her very favorite cereal of all time.

"Hailey will pay you back for the nail polish," my mom says.

"Those are very beautiful shoes," I tell my mom. This is called distracting. Because I cannot pay Kaitlyn back. I do not have any money. I do not have a job. And I spent my allowance already. And me and Russ have not had a lemonade stand in forever and ever.

"Hailey," my mom says. "Today after my meeting I will bring you over to Aunt Denise's house. You and Cousin Angela will clean out Uncle Adam's car to earn money to buy Kaitlyn new nail polish."

I gasp. "But I did not even spill that nail polish or use it!"

"Then how come your pinkie nail is painted blue?" Kaitlyn asks.

Oops.

Chapter Five

- -

A Job at Aunt
Denise's House

I do not have time to think about having a job later at Cousin Angela's house. And that is because I am trying to figure out a way to sneak that dress off to school.

"Why are we in your mom and dad's room?" Maybelle asks. We are tip, tip, tiptoeing quiet as a mouse into my mom and dad's bedroom. My mom and dad's bedroom is off-limits. But there is no choice. My flower girl dress is in here.

"Shhh!" I tell Maybelle. Even though no one can hear her, she should be very quiet. We are on a secret mission. I take that beautiful blue dress out of the closet. Then I go into the hall and try to quick run into my room. But before I can get there, I go running right into my dad. Uh-oh.

"Hailey," he says. "What were you doing in our room?"

"Just moving my dress into my own room," I tell him. This is not a lie. I am moving it into my own room. But I do not tell him that I am wearing it to school. And I do not tell him that my mom did not tell me to move that dress.

"Okay," my dad says. "Have a good day at school." Dads are good when you are trying to do something that you do not have a permission to do. And that is because they do not ask too many questions. They are in their own world.

"You have a good day, too!" I say very happy.

Then I am run, run, running back to my room. And I am pulling on my flower girl dress. And I am putting it on right over my jeans and T-shirt! The sleeves of my T-shirt are a little sticking out. But it still looks very beautiful.

"You better put that dress back, Hailey!" Maybelle says. "You are going to make a big mess of it. It is looking very stretchy over the clothes you are wearing."

"It is okay," I tell her. "I am going to be very careful." I am tuck, tuck, tucking the bottom of my dress right into my pants.

I put a nice big heavy coat on over that dress. To cover it all right up.

I get my book bag. And I take my lunch box out of the fridge.

"Good-bye, Kaitlyn," I say. "It is time for me to leave for school."

"Good-bye," she says. She does not sound

like she really cares too much. She is still mad about that nail polish. But she will get over it.

"Good-bye, Mom and Dad, I am going to be late for the bus so I will see you later!" I yell up the stairs. And then I go running out to the bus stop.

- -

When I get to school I am causing quite a spectacle. A spectacle is when you cause a big scene and people pay a lot of very good attention to you. Being a spectacle is fun. It is like being famous.

"Hailey!" Addie Jokobeck gasps when she sees me. Her eyes get big, big, big like two round beach balls. "You are wearing a fancy dress."

"Yup!" I say. "I am!" I hang my coat up in the back of room four on my special hook. I did not have my flower crown ready yet. Cousin Genevieve is going to buy them right on the wedding day.

But that is not even a problem. On account of how I picked some flowers from the outside of school. And then made them into a crown.

"I made you a flower crown, too," I tell Addie Jokobeck. I plop it onto her head. "You look very beautiful, Addie." I clap my hands and twirl around in my dress. "Do you see how fluttery this dress is?"

"Yes." Addie Jokobeck is touching her crown. It is getting a little bit tangled all up in her hair. Oh, well. She can use some scissors to cut it out later if it gets too stuck.

"Uh-oh," Maybelle says. "Here comes Natalie Brice."

Natalie Brice is coming in. And Natalie

Brice is holding something in her hand. And that something is a camera!

"Cameras are not allowed in school, Natalie Brice," I tell her. I am keeping my voice very sweet. And that is because I want her to notice my beautiful princess wedding dress.

"Yes, they are," she says.

"No, they are not."

"Well, I am just going to show you a picture of me in my beautiful dress." She puts that screen of the camera right in Addie Jokobeck's face. And she says, "See, Addie, I had a jewel crown. With real diamonds that cost thousands of dollars."

I look over Addie's shoulder at that picture. Natalie is wearing a beautiful dress! And a jewel crown! With real diamonds that cost thousands of dollars!

"Look at my flower crown!" I yell. "Everyone in room four look at the flower crown that Hailey Twitch is wearing."

Some people turn to look. That is when the spectacle part really starts.

"That flower crown is wilted and ugly," Natalie says. She wrinkles her nose right up and looks at me like I smell like old garbage.

"It is not," I tell her. "And Addie Jokobeck has one, too."

"Hers is wilted and ugly, too," Natalie says.

"It is not! These flower crowns are gorgeous."

But Addie Jokobeck does not look so sure. She is trying to pull her flower crown right off her head. And she is looking like maybe she thinks it is ugly and wilted.

"You stole those flowers from outside," Natalie says. And then she decides to be a big tattletale. "Miss Stephanie!" she says. "Hailey Twitch stole some flowers from outside of the school, and she put them on her head."

"No, I did not," I say. I am keeping my voice very calm. I quick cross my fingers behind my back, and then I say a little fib. "We have these same flowers at home. The same ones that are right at this school."

"Hailey," Miss Stephanie says. "What is that you are wearing?"

"Thank you for noticing, Miss Stephanie." I do another big twirl. I am hoping maybe

Antonio Fuerte will notice how fancy I am looking. So far he is in the corner playing trucks and not paying too much attention. "This is a very amazing flower girl dress that I am going to wear when I am a flower girl."

"Does your mother know you wore that dress to school?" Miss Stephanie asks.

"Yes, of course." That is another fib. "She says it is okay as long as I am very, very careful and do not spill anything on it like marker or paint or food."

"Hailey." Miss Stephanie sighs. "Please come with me."

- -

Miss Stephanie takes me right down to the main office!

"Do I have to go and see the principal?" I ask as we are walking down there.

"No," Miss Stephanie says. "But I do want

us to call your mom and make sure that you are allowed to be wearing that dress." Her shoes are making clacking noises on the hallway. *Clack, clack, clack.* She is having a teacher's aide watch our class. It is a very big mess of a situation, if you want to know the truth.

"Uh-oh," Maybelle says. She is flying all around my head. "Someone is going to be in very big trouble and that someone is you."

"Miss Stephanie," I say. "My mom is in a very important meeting, and she cannot come to the phone right now." I shrug. "Sorry, it is out of my hands."

But Miss Stephanie is not listening. She is in the main office, and she is asking the secretary for my mom's phone number right away. And then she is calling her! She is dialing that number immediately. And then she is asking right away if I am allowed to be wearing that dress.

"What did she say?" I whisper when Miss Stephanie is hanging up the office phone.

"She said she is coming to bring you some different clothes."

- -

My mom is very, very, very mad. On account of how I wore that dress to school. And on account of how she had to bring me new clothes and miss her very big important meeting.

This day is getting worse and worse. Especially after school when I have to go work at Aunt Denise's house.

"Hello, Hailey," Aunt Denise says when she opens the door. "Come on in."

My mom is coming in, too. Her and Aunt Denise are going to sit in the kitchen and drink coffee and eat cake while me and Cousin Angela are working our butts off. That does not sound like a very fair plan.

"I hope we are not going to be doing any yard work," I say. "I hate yard work." Yard work is very hard because you get dirty and you have to use a wheelbarrow. I know all about it because one time I had to do some yard work for my neighbor Mr. Frisk. He is very old. Maybe even one hundred. And so he cannot do yard work all by his own self.

"Today you are going to be cleaning out Uncle Adam's car," Aunt Denise says. She holds out one trash bag to me. And one trash bag to Cousin Angela. Cousin Angela takes the bag. She is picking her nose.

"That girl is very gross," Maybelle says. "She is always picking her nose."

Me and Cousin Angela go outside. I am hoping this is going to be an easy job. But when we open that car door, it is a very big disaster area! Uncle Adam's car is even worse than Kaitlyn's room! And Kaitlyn's room is the biggest mess I ever saw in my whole life.

Cousin Angela holds her nose. "That car

smells," she says. Then she drops her trash bag right on the driveway. She picks up a jump rope and starts skipping right away. Skip, skip, skip.

"Maybelle," I whisper. "Do something about this!"

"About what?" Maybelle asks. She is sitting on the hood of the car. Doing nothing.

"About me having to do all this work all by my own self," I say.

"What should I do about it?" Maybelle asks.

I sigh. I have to think of everything around here. "You could break that jump rope right in half."

Maybelle looks over at Cousin Angela. And she pulls out her wand. And then she makes that jump rope all sparkly, and suddenly Cousin Angela is going faster and faster and jumping all over.

"Maybelle!" I whisper. "I said to break that jump rope right in half. Not make it go faster."

"Sorry." She gives a big shrug. "I guess I am not so good at magic."

It is a very big lie. She is pretending not to be good at magic so that Mr. Tuttle will not send her back to the castle.

I think about maybe having a big fit or a tantrum. Or maybe I will go inside and be a big tattletale. But then I have a fab, fab, fabulous idea.

"Oh, Cousin Angela," I call right over to her. "I have a great idea for you!"

"What?" She sticks her finger right up in her nose again.

"How would you like it if I clean out this whole car, and you do not even have to do one thing? That is called not even having to lift a finger!"

She thinks about it. "So you will be my servant?"

"Yes. I will be your servant." I do a big sigh. "And if I am your servant, then that means that I have to clean this whole car. And it means that you will not have to be a flower girl! Because I will have to do the whole job for you." I put a fake sad face on. "That will be a really hard job, but I will have to do it because I am your servant."

"No!" Cousin Angela screams. She starts swinging the jump rope around her head. "I am the flower girl!" Yikes. She is getting closer and closer with that rope.

"But if you aren't the flower girl, then you don't have to clean out the car." I am moving back, back, back quick as I can. Because that rope is swinging very close to me. It is making me a little nervous if you want to know the whole truth and nothing but the truth.

"I AM GOING TO BE THE FLOWER GIRL!" Cousin Angela is screaming.

And that is when I lose it.

"MOM!" I yell. I am running all across the lawn like a crazy person. "MOM, AUNT DENISE, COUSIN GENIEVIEVE, PLEASE

SOMEONE COME OUT HERE AND SAVE ME FROM THIS ROPE!"

My mom comes running out onto the porch. "Girls!" she says. "What is all this yelling about?"

"Cousin Angela is chasing me with a jump rope!" I say. I am still running all around the yard. My hands are waving all in the air. But

when I look behind me, Cousin Angela is not even chasing me one bit.

She is standing in the driveway. She is holding a trash bag. And she is cleaning out Uncle Adam's car.

"Hailey, what are you talking about?" Aunt Denise asks. She is out on the porch now, too. So is Cousin Genevieve. They are all looking at me like I am maybe a little bit crazy in my head.

"Cousin Angela was chasing me around with a jump rope." I point over to the rope. But it is just sitting on the driveway now. Like it is no big deal.

"Angela!" Aunt Denise calls. "Is that true?"

"Is what true, Mommy?" Cousin Angela asks. She is dropping an old paper cup into her garbage bag.

"Did you chase Hailey around the yard with a jump rope?"

"No, Mommy," Cousin Angela says. She

shakes her head no, no, no. "I was just cleaning out the car."

"Are you sure, Angela?" Aunt Denise asks.

"Yes." She is nodding up and down. "But there is one thing that happened. And that is that Hailey told me that if I did not stop being a flower girl, then she would tell you that I chased her around with a jump rope."

"What?!" I shriek. "That is a big fat lie, Cousin Angela, and you know it!"

"YEAH!" Maybelle says. She puts her hands right on her hips and gives a mean look to Cousin Angela.

"Hailey, please stop yelling at me," Cousin Angela says. And then she drops her garbage bag on the ground. And bursts right into tears.

And I get stuck cleaning Uncle Adam's car out all by my own self.

Chapter Six

Get Them off My Feet

After I am done cleaning out that disgusting, gross, horrible car, it is time to go and look at shoes. Perfect, sparkly, beautiful shoes! Just like Dorothy from this one movie I know called *The Wizard of Oz*. Only that girl Dorothy's shoes are red. And mine are going to be pink, pink, pink!

"Oh," the saleslady says when she sees me. "You again." She does not look too happy to see me. That is not very polite.

"Yes, it is us again!" I say. "We are here to get some wonderful sparkly shoes. So please show me the shoes for flower girls." Now I am old enough to know that there are shoes for brides and shoes for flower girls. I am not going to make that mistake again.

"Here are the shoes for the flower girls," the saleslady says. "Let me know if you need any help." She is looking at us with a very nervous look on her face. I think she is scared we are going to cause a big scene.

"These are the ones!" I pick up the sparkly shoes. "I would like these in my size, please."

The saleslady asks the sizes of me and Cousin Angela. Then she goes to get those shoes.

When she comes back, I slide my feet into those shoes right away. They are a little bit pinchy in the toes. But I do not care. They are very perfect. Better than Natalie Brice's jewel crown even.

I am looking at myself in these very wonderful little foot mirrors. I cannot get enough of it. "These shoes are the most beautiful shoes in the world," I tell Cousin Angela. "Do you love them?"

Cousin Angela is looking down at herself in those shoes. She is walking around. She is putting her hand on her hip. She is looking in the foot mirror. And then all of a sudden she is screaming.

"THESE SHOES ARE STUPID!"

"Cousin Angela," I say real quick, trying to calm her down. "Just relax. See how nice and pretty these shoes are? They look like just the kind of shoes a flower girl would wear."

"I DON'T LIKE SPARKLES!"

I gasp. That is impossible. Everyone loves sparkles. You cannot *not* love sparkles. This is not making any kind of sense in my head.

Aunt Denise and my mom think this is the most hilarious thing they have ever seen in their lives. They are laughing their heads right off.

"This is not a laughing matter," I tell them. "Please try to be mature about it."

But this makes them just laugh even harder.

"Hailey," my mom says. "You and Cousin Angela have to pick a shoe that you both like."

"I don't like these ones!" Cousin Angela says.

And then Maybelle does something very bad. She swoops right down in front of Cousin Angela. And she points her wand at those sparkly shoes.

"Maybelle," I whisper. "What did you just do? I do not have time to clean up any more of your messes."

"These shoes are tight on my feet," Cousin Angela says. "I want them off this instant!" She plops herself right down on the floor of that store. And then she tries to take those shoes right off. She tugs. And she tugs. But those shoes will not come off.

"Looks like we will have to buy them," I say. "Since they will not come off your feet."

"GET THEM OFF MY FEET, MOMMY!"

"I am sorry, but if you cannot keep your children quiet, you will have to leave this store," the lady who works there says.

"Yes, I'm sorry, but we cannot stay quiet," I say. "We are very loud and bad. Now we would like two pairs of these shoes, please. Wrap them up to go." I point at those sparkle shoes. "And then we will be out of here. And not be causing a big scene anymore."

"OW, MY FEET, OW!" Cousin Angela is really having a bad screaming fit now. She is pounding her feet right on the ground.

"Calm down, Angela," Aunt Denise says. She is down trying to pull those shoes off Cousin Angela. But they will not come off. "What size are these shoes?" Aunt Denise is saying. "They are stuck on your foot."

I look at Maybelle. She is sitting in a big bride shoe that has a big fat bow on it. "Maybelle," I whisper. "What did you do to that shoe?"

"She cannot get it off," Maybelle says, giving me a big smile. "That is me using bad magic. And that is you getting those shoes."

I love that sprite! She is always coming through for me.

Now my mom and Cousin Genevieve are over trying to help get that shoe off Cousin Angela. So I put my sparkly shoes on. And I start to play a skipping game. I grab a bride veil off of a shelf and put it right over my head.

"Yes, I will marry you, Antonio," I say. "But only if we can live in my house with my mom and dad and Kaitlyn."

"Angela, hold still!" Aunt Denise is saying.

She is pulling on the top of that shoe. And my mom is pulling on the bottom. But that shoe will still not come off. It just does not want to budge.

"Well," I say real loud, "I guess we will have to buy those shoes. And Cousin Angela will have to wear them everywhere until it is time for the wedding."

I am still playing a skipping game. No one is paying any attention to me.

"I do," I say into the mirror. I am pretending I am a bride. And I am marrying Antonio Fuerte. I start to sing a very good wedding song I know and twirl all around. "Dum dum da dummmmm."

Rrrrrippp. Uh-oh. I look down. I accidentally stepped on that veil. And now there is a big rip in it. There is another sign on the wall here. And that sign says YOU BREAK IT, YOU BUY IT. Yikes.

"Maybelle," I whisper. "Please come and fix this veil immediately."

But I forgot about Maybelle trying to be bad at her magic. On account of tricking Mr. Tuttle. And so when Maybelle points her wand, that veil rips even more.

"Guess I'll just return this headdress back where I found it," I say real loud in case anyone is listening. I put it right back down on the shelf. "It is exactly like it was when I picked it up, perfect and beautiful."

"Owwww!" Cousin Angela is screaming. "THEY'RE PINCHING! THESE SHOES ARE PINCHING!"

"They are not," Aunt Denise says. She finally pulls one of them off. *Pop!* She looks in the shoe. "I don't understand. They're your right size. Why are they so small?"

"That is very weird," I say, shrugging. "Well, anyway, that situation is all over now. And I still think we should buy them. They are very beautiful shoes."

"Excuse me," the saleslady says. I turn around. She is holding up that ripped headdress!

"No," I say quickly. "We do not need a headdress veil today. But we will take two of these pairs of sparkly shoes. And we are in a very big hurry, so hop to it." Then I remember my manners. "Please."

"Hailey!" my mom says. "What did you do to that veil?"

"I did not do one thing to that headdress," I say. I look at it real close. "I have never seen that headdress in my life."

"You were wearing it around and singing," the saleslady says. "And then you ripped it."

"How much is it?" my mom asks. She is looking very pale in her face.

"Three hundred dollars," the lady says.

"Three hundred dollars!" I yell. "That thing is a rip-off!"

"I think," Aunt Denise says, "that it is time to go."

- -

Chapter Seven

A Permission for Maybelle

My mom is very mad at me. She gave me the silent treatment all the way home. She is probably going to think up a very bad punishment for me. On account of how I wore my dress to school. And on account of how I ripped that headdress.

I decide that I will do something very good to make up for it. First I clean my room all up. I put all my toys away. I put all my books on my shelf very neat. I pick up all my clothes and put them in my hamper. I even put all my puzzles away very perfect, instead of just shoving them into their boxes in a big jumble of a mess.

Then I sit down at my desk.

Here is what I pull out:

One piece of plain white paper.

One bottle of silvery glitter.

One glue stick.

Some sparkly heart stickers.

Four gel pens.

"I AM SORRY" I write on the front of the paper. Then I fold it in half to make a wonderful card. And on the inside of that card I write "I LOVE YOU, FROM HAILEY."

I put some beautiful sparkly red heart stickers on it. And then comes the very best part.

I cover that whole card with my glue stick. And then sprinkle sparkly silver glitter all over it.

"What is that?" Maybelle asks. Some glitter is flying up in the air and getting all over her wings.

"That is an 'I'm sorry' card for my mom." I am getting glitter all over the place. I brush it off my hands. Glitter goes flying up and up and up into the air. Maybelle has a big sneeze.

"Ah-choo!" She waves her hand in front of her face.

"It is the most perfect card I ever made," I tell her. "My mom will be so happy when she sees it. She will forget all about that headdress. And then she—"

I do not get to finish what I am saying. Because all of a sudden, there is a flash of blue lightning! A flash of blue lightning that can only mean one thing!

"Mr. Tuttle!" I say as he pops right up in my room. "What are you doing here?" I am getting a little bit nervous. Mr. Tuttle looks like a principal. He has a big stomach and glasses and a mustache. And he is in charge of Maybelle. He is not very fun or funny.

"I have come to tell Maybelle she will be going back to the castle on Saturday." Mr. Tuttle makes a mark right down on his clipboard. He is always writing important facts down on that thing.

"Saturday is impossible," I tell him. "We are going to a wedding on that day, thank you very much." I shrug my shoulders. "Sorry, it is out of my hands."

"Maybelle can go to the wedding," Mr. Tuttle says. "But she will be leaving right after that."

I go over and sprinkle some glitter right onto his bald head. "There you go," I say, patting him on the shoulder. "You need a little sparkle in your life."

Mr. Tuttle does not like that. "I will be back on Saturday," he says.

"If you say so," I say. "But if I were you, I would keep an eye on that Maybelle. She is turning into a disaster with her magic."

"What do you mean?" Mr. Tuttle is raising up his eyebrows and looking very interested in this.

"I mean that she glued some shoes right onto my cousin Angela's feet."

"Is that true, Maybelle?" Mr. Tuttle seems very shocked.

"Yes," Maybelle says. "My magic is a big mess."

She is a very good actress, that Maybelle. She should be a movie star for sprites.

"Well, I will be keeping an eye on you," Mr. Tuttle says. "And if you have a good handle on your magic, then you will go back to the castle with me on Saturday."

And then he is gone.

"Don't worry," I tell her. "You will get to stay. You just have to keep doing bad things. Now let's go give this card to my mom."

My mom is very happy about that card. She loves it more than anything in her whole life. She is very glad that I said I am sorry.

But she still says I am going to have to have a punishment. And then there is more bad news. And that bad news is sitting right on the kitchen table.

"What are those?" I am wrinkling up my nose at those plain shoes that are sitting there. They are white. With no sparkles. No glitter. Not even one bow!

"Those are the shoes you and Cousin Angela are going to be wearing in the wedding," my mom says.

"First of all, shoes are not allowed to be sitting on the table, thank you very much." I put those shoes right on the floor. "And second of all, I am going to be wearing sparkly shoes only."

"No," my mom says. "You are not."

"Yes, I am."

"No, you are not. And if you make a fit about it, you are going to get a bigger punishment."

What a disaster of a wedding.

- - - - - - - - - - - - - - - - - -

Chapter Eight

A Couple of Disasters

The rest of that week goes by very slow. It is going slow, slow, slow, slow, slow up until that wedding.

But on Friday in music class we are allowed to have free music again. And this time I am running up and grabbing those bongo drums right out of the box.

"Did you get your sparkly shoes yet?" Natalie Brice asks. She is using the pipe instrument. That is the second best instrument to have.

"Not yet," I say. This is not even really a lie. Because I do not have them yet. But I will figure something out. I am good at figuring things out right at the last minute.

"But you're getting them, right?"

"Of course I am getting them. What kind of wedding do you think this is?"

"Sometimes you lie about things. A lot of things."

I give her a mean look. "Well, I am not lying about this."

We all fall into a line. And we make wonderful music all together as a class.

Then Mr. Green says, "This is our last day of the music unit. So please put your instruments back into the bucket until next year."

This is wrong. We are supposed to be able to keep those instruments for our own selves! Just like last year's class. And I need those bongo drums. So that I can make music at the wedding. And if I put them back in that bucket, that mean one Natalie Brice will snatch them right up.

So I just sit real quiet in my seat. Everyone else is putting their instruments back in the bucket. But I will not do it. I am going to keep these perfect bongo drums right in my lap, thank you very much.

"Hailey Twitch," Mr. Green says. "Will you please put the bongos back into the instrument bucket?"

"No, that is okay." I set those bongos down very carefully on my desk. This is so Mr. Green will know that I am going to take very good care of them. They are going to a great home.

"No?" Mr. Green looks very confused. He does a big frown, and a big wrinkle comes on his forehead. Then he sighs and smooths his hair back. "Would you like to tell me why not, please?"

"Because I am going to bring these bongo drums home," I say. I hold them up and play them. *Boom, boom, boom.* That beautiful sound is music to my ears.

"Hailey," Mr. Green says. He closes his eyes like he cannot even deal with this. "You cannot take those drums home. They belong to the music department."

"But when we are done with the instruments, we get to take them home," I tell him. "And I would like to pick these bongo drums, please." I give him a very good smile.

"No, you do not get to take them home."

"Last year they did."

"That is because last year we got all new instruments. And so the students were allowed to take the old ones home. Now please return the drums to the instrument bucket."

This whole room is acting very quiet. No one is talking. Or whispering. All they are doing is staring. Right at me. They are staring right at me while I am getting up from my desk. They are staring right at me when I am walking over to the instrument corner. They are staring right at me when I am putting those drums back into the instrument bucket. They are staring right at me when I am walking back to my desk.

Except for Natalie Brice. She is staring, too. But she is also laughing.

- -

"That Natalie Brice thinks she is the boss of everything!" I yell to Maybelle when I am walking home from the bus stop. "She is a no good traitor." I am not exactly sure what a traitor is. But I know it is something very, very bad.

"Hello, Mr. Frisk," I say when I am walking by his house. Mr. Frisk is our neighbor. He has very bushy eyebrows. And he is bald. He is very nice. But sometimes I bother him. And then he puts a sign on his door that says PLEASE DO NOT DISTURB. That is how I know that I am not supposed to knock on his door. Mr. Frisk likes his quiet time.

"Hi, Hailey." Mr. Frisk is sitting out on his porch and drinking a cup of coffee. But I do not have time to see him today. That is because I have to go to the important rehearsal dinner tonight.

A rehearsal dinner is when you practice the wedding. So that nothing bad will happen.

"I am ready to go to that rehearsal!" I yell as I go bursting into my house. "Get out the dress! I am ready to put it on." I tear off my coat and throw it on the floor.

"Hailey," my mom says. "Please pick up your coat and hang it in the closet."

I go and pick my coat up. I hang it in the closet real careful.

Then I walk very calm over to where my mom is sitting on the couch. "I am ready to put my dress on now," I say. I sit down next to her very soft. I cross my hands over my legs. That is so she will know I am not too overexcited and hyper.

"I'm glad you're ready for the rehearsal," my mom says. "But it is not until seven o'clock. And you are not going to be wearing your dress."

I jump off that couch right away. "What do you mean about that dress?"

"You won't wear the dress to the rehearsal," my mom says. "You will only wear it tomorrow at the wedding."

"But this dinner is supposed to be like a practice. And I need my dress to practice." I wonder if my mom has ever heard of this thing called a dress rehearsal. It is when you get all dressed up in your outfit and you practice. I did it once for this play I was in called *The Gingerbread Princess*.

"You cannot wear your dress," my mom says. "And that is that."

- -

The rehearsal, it turns out, is not going to be very fun or funny. We are not allowed to wear our flower girl dresses. And we have to sit in a very fancy room. And everyone has to be very quiet. And eat this very fancy dinner. And that is all before we can even practice walking down the aisle. This is a very big waste of time.

I have to sit at the end of the table. With Cousin Angela.

"Something very bad is going to be happening at this dinner," Maybelle says. She is drinking some apple juice out of a very fancy glass.

"I do not like this food," Cousin Angela says.

"Me neither." I am poking at the food. It is some kind of big piece of meat. And it looks very slimy and gross.

"That is filet mignon," Cousin Harold says. Cousin Harold is Cousin Genevieve's brother. He has a lot, lot, lot of freckles, and he is as skinny as a flagpole. He is sitting right across from us.

"What's your name again?" Cousin Angela asks him. She is kneeling up on her chair instead of sitting flat. "I forget your name."

"That's Cousin Harold," I tell her. Then I roll my eyes at Cousin Harold. "Aren't kids just the cutest?" I ask him.

"I WANT ONE OF THOSE ROLLS!" Angela says.

Cousin Harold passes her one.

"What are those spots all over your face?" Cousin Angela asks Harold.

"Those are freckles," I tell her. "They are very beautiful orange spots."

Cousin Harold's face goes very red, red, red. But you can still see those orange spots.

"Your face is turning red," Cousin Angela

says. She opens up her roll and licks some butter right out of it.

I am keeping my roll closed in half while I eat it. I am crossing my fingers for someone to notice that I am eating very neat. Then they will see that I am very mature and ready to be a flower girl. And that Cousin Angela is very much too young to be doing such an important job.

"I am glad that I am not licking butter out of my roll!" I say real loud.

"This meat is yucky." Angela pushes her plate right out of the way. "It is bloody meat."

Cousin Harold gasps. Then he turns away from us and starts talking to the person next to him.

"You are right," I tell Cousin Angela. "That

meat is gross. Maybe you should ask for a hamburger and make a big fit about it."

"Why?" she asks. She is looking at me very suspicious.

"Because it is bloody meat. Like you just said." I wrinkle up my nose. I make a very gross face at her. So she knows that meat is yuck, yuck, yucky. "Time to have a good tantrum!" I say really happy.

That is called encouragement. Encouragement is when you tell someone they can do something. Like in gym class when we run the three-legged race. I am always partners with Russ Robertson. And I say to him, "Come on, Russ, let's go! We cannot let that mean one Natalie Brice beat us!"

Sometimes encouragement does not work. Like when Russ tries to go faster. And his legs get tangled up, and we fall on the gym floor, and he gets a bloody lip.

"I do not want to have a fit," Cousin Angela says. "I just want chicken nuggets."

Maybelle gets a very happy look on her face. Then she points her wand right at Cousin Angela's plate. And before I even know what is happening, there are chicken nuggets on it! And French fries. And one glass of soda. It looks very delicious-o.

"Maybelle," I whisper. "Please make me some of those nuggets, please."

But Maybelle gives a shrug of her shoulders. "Sorry, Hailey," she says. "But I cannot control my magic."

"Where is my meat?" Cousin Angela says. And then she bursts right into tears. She is crying very loud. And getting wet tears all over her napkin.

"What is wrong, Angela?" Aunt Denise is asking.

"I think she is scared of Harold's spots," I say. "She does not like freckles too much."

"Hailey!" my dad says.

"What? I love freckles. They are very beautiful." I turn to Cousin Harold. "Sorry if I hurt your feelings, Cousin Harold. But you should love those gorgeous freckles. If I had all those freckles, I would take a marker and connect the dots."

"Hailey!" my mom says.

"HAILEY TOLD ME I SHOULD HAVE A FIT!" Cousin Angela yells. She is push, push, pushing her chair back. Then she gets out of it. And then she starts running all around that big fancy table.

"Where did those chicken nuggets come from?" Aunt Denise is asking. "And that soda? Angela, you know you are not supposed to be drinking sugar."

"I LOVE SUGAR!" Cousin Angela yells. Now Cousin Harold is out of his chair. And he is chasing Angela all around the table. They are running and running.

"Those two are making me dizzy," Maybelle says.

"Very dizzy," I say.

And that is when it happens. A waiter comes out of the kitchen. He is holding a tray of very good and fancy desserts. And Cousin Angela goes slamming right into him.

"Ahhhhh!" the waiter screams.

Desserts are flying all over the place. Some frosting gets on Cousin Angela's hair and face.

"Wow," I say. "What a mess she made. Sometimes five-year-olds can really be a big pain. On account of how they are so young."

The waiter is looking down at Cousin Angela. He is looking down at all the desserts.

"Are you okay, little girl?" he asks.

Cousin Angela is looking like maybe she is going to cry some more. I start to feel very sad in my heart. Because I did not want her to get hurt.

"Are you hurt, Cousin Angela?" I ask. I am getting out of my chair and kneeling down right by her side. But Cousin Angela just looks at me. Then she reaches over and picks a big piece of chocolate cake up with her hand. Then she takes a bite. And then she reaches out and smears that cake all over my face.

Chapter Nine

- -

Kaitlyn to the Rescue

"That was a disaster of a dinner," I say when we get home. Kaitlyn is sitting in the living room. She is watching a scary movie on TV. Kaitlyn is only allowed to watch scary movies when I am not home. This is because of something having to do with a scary movie that made me want to sleep with my mom and dad for two whole weeks.

That happened all the way last year when I was six. I am ready for scary movies now. But no one will give me a second chance.

"What happened?" Kaitlyn asks.

"Cousin Angela was very bad, and she slammed into a waiter, and a big thing of chocolate cake went all over, and then she smeared it all on my face."

"That does sound like a disaster," Kaitlyn agrees. "Did you get to practice walking down the aisle?"

"Yes, after dinner. And after I washed all that cake off my face." The part was very fun. I had to do a special wedding walk. I am going to use that special wedding walk tomorrow when I am wearing my beautiful dress. "And guess what else?" I ask Kaitlyn.

"What?"

"Today in school Natalie Brice made fun of me."

"Natalie Brice is mean," Kaitlyn says.

"Yes, she is very mean."

"Why did she make fun of you?"

"Because I thought that I was allowed to keep this one instrument. But it turned out to be a big misunderstanding."

"What kind of instrument?" Kaitlyn asks.

"A very wonderful pair of bongo drums. I had a very good plan to play those drums at the wedding tomorrow."

"I have some bongo drums," Kaitlyn says. She is sitting up on the couch. "They are left over from a Hawaiian birthday party I went to. You can have them."

My mouth drops open. Because that news is very much too good to be true.

But then Kaitlyn takes me up to her room. And she pulls out one pair of bongo drums! One pair that are perfect and amazing and exactly what I wanted.

"Just please do not play them all night." Kaitlyn puts her hands on her head. "That will give me a headache." That is called exaggerating. Kaitlyn is a drama queen. But she is a very nice drama queen. And a very nice sister.

"I won't," I promise.

And then Kaitlyn spends the rest of the night braiding my hair. And she even lets me do hers, too.

— — — — — — — — — — — — — — — — — —

The next morning is the wedding, and so I am up very early.

"Hello, morning!" I say. I pull, pull, pull the curtains on my window right open. "Hello, Mr. Frisk!" I shout down to him. He is picking up his newspaper from the bottom of his driveway.

"Hailey, please stop with all that yelling," he says. "You are going to wake up the whole neighborhood."

"But, Mr. Frisk, I am going to be in a wedding today." I am still yelling.

"Oh." Mr. Frisk looks a little bit interested in this news. "Well, have fun. And make sure you behave."

"I will."

"What kind of dress will I wear?" Maybelle asks. She is pointing her wand right at her own self. And whipping up all kinds of fab, fab, fabulous dresses. The first one is yellow. Then one is red. Then one is pink.

"You are going to wear the same dress as me," I tell her. "That way me and you will be twins." I have always wanted to be a twin with someone. But not Cousin Angela. I am thinking maybe I can pretend Addie Jokobeck is my twin. Maybe she will go along with it. I think that story could really catch on.

Maybelle points her wand. And then she is wearing the same dress as me!

"You look very beautiful," I tell her. Then I turn toward the door. "Mom!" I yell. "MOM, COME IN HERE RIGHT NOW! IT IS TIME TO PUT MY DRESS ON."

My mom comes running in. She is wearing rollers in her hair.

"Yes, Hailey," she says. "But first you have to take a bath."

Ugh. I hate baths. But I take one so I can get this show on the road. After my bath I have to get my hair done in a very fancy way of a French braid. Then Kaitlyn paints my nails a very beautiful pink. And I even get to wear one swipe of lip gloss!

And then it is finally time to put on that dress. It is just perfect like I remember.

The only thing is that those shoes are still very boring. But I am thinking there is still one way to maybe make them have some sparkles. And that is with my special glitter pen!

But I cannot paint those shoes right now. And that is because my dad is around. And my mom. And Kaitlyn.

"What are you doing with that glitter pen, Hailey?" Maybelle is asking me. Maybelle thinks she is so smart. On account of that she gave herself some beautiful glitter shoes.

"That is for me to know and you to find out." I put that glitter pen right in my special wedding purse. And then it is time to leave for the wedding!

Chapter Ten

The Wedding at Last

The wedding is going to be in a very big church.

And everyone that is in the wedding is allowed to go right into the back. Into a special room. But only if you are a VIP. That stands for Very Important Person. And I am one of them.

"Hello, Hailey," Cousin Angela says. "Guess what?"

"What?"

"I counted Cousin Harold's freckles, and he has eleventy seventy-five of them."

I do a big sigh. Cousin Angela does not know how to count so well.

Then there is a big commotion that is

coming from the back of the room. Something is happening with Cousin Genevieve's veil. She has lost that veil! All the grown-ups are getting very upset about this.

They are not paying any attention to me.

So this is the perfect time to make my shoes all very sparkly!

I sit down in a corner. And I pull those plain white shoes right off my feet.

"Do you think I should make my socks sparkly, too?" I ask Maybelle. Then I wiggle my toes. I am wearing very fancy lacy socks.

"I think that might be going too far," Maybelle says.

"I think you might be right."

I get to work coloring in those shoes. They are looking very beautiful and sparkly. I put them back on.

"Look at those sparkles!" I say to Maybelle. "They look very dashing!"

"Gorgeous!" Maybelle says.

Finally the grown-ups find Cousin Genevieve's veil! Somehow it was behind a big box. They brush some dust off it.

Then it is time to finally walk down the aisle. Just like we practiced last night after that disaster of a dinner.

Cousin Angela and I stand at the end of the aisle.

We are holding our baskets of rose petals, ready to go.

"Hey," Cousin Angela says. She is looking down at my shoes. "Why are your shoes all sparkly?"

"I colored them sparkly," I say. "With a

sparkly marker. So it is all settled. Your shoes are not sparkly, like you wanted. And my shoes are sparkly. That is called compromising."

But Cousin Angela does not look happy. Her face is looking very stormy. She is looking like I do right before it is time to have a good long fit.

"I WANT SPARKLY SHOES!" Cousin Angela screams.

I am shocked by this news. "But you said you hate sparkles. Remember?" I pat her on the head. "Now come on, time to walk down the aisle and get this wedding going."

"NO!" she shrieks. "I want sparkles right now!"

"Maybelle," I whisper. "Please give Cousin Angela some sparkly shoes." I am hoping that this wedding will not be a big wreck. But Maybelle does not want to use her magic for good. So she points her wand out. And when she pulls it back, Cousin Angela's shoes are bright orange!

"I HATE ORANGE!" Cousin Angela screams.

I take her hand. "Come on," I say. "It is time to walk down the aisle. We will talk about this later."

"NO!"

One of the church ladies is whispering right to us. "Girls," she says. "Start to walk, please."

I start to walk. And finally so does Cousin Angela.

Everyone in the seats is watching us. It is like being a very famous movie star. I give my best smile. There is Grandma Hansen. And Aunt Denise. And my mom and dad and Kaitlyn. They are taking lots of pictures of me.

I am having a very fun time at this wedding, it turns out.

But then all of a sudden, everyone in the audience is not looking so happy. They are looking very worried.

"THESE SHOES ARE UGLY!" Cousin Angela yells. Then she sits right down in the aisle. And she kicks her legs right up in the air. One of her orange shoes goes up, up, up! And it plops down right on Cousin Harold's head.

"Ow!" Cousin Harold says. Wow. I hope he does not have a scrape on his head. I do not like blood. It makes me very nervous.

"Come on, honey," Aunt Denise says. She is getting out of her seat. She is putting her hand out to Cousin Angela. "Time to walk down the aisle like a good flower girl."

"NO!" Cousin Angela screams. She is pulling off her other shoe. Then she throws it right at Kaitlyn. Kaitlyn catches it.

"Good catch, Kaitlyn!" I say. But she does not smile. Or give me a high five. She just looks very upset. So does my mom. And my dad. And everyone else that is watching. The wonderful music is even stopping. This is definitely not going according to plan.

I decide it is time to save this wedding. "Come on," I say to Cousin Angela. "Chop, chop!"

But Cousin Angela is still yelling and screaming. "I AM QUITTING THIS WEDDING!"

"Haha," Aunt Denise says. She is giving a weird laugh. "Come on, Angela." She picks Cousin Angela up and puts her right over her shoulder like a big sack of potatoes! Then she takes her back into the VIP room. Wow. This wedding is the biggest disaster I ever saw.

"Hailey," Maybelle whispers. "You are the flower girl now! The only one!"

I gasp. She is right! I am the only flower girl. In sparkly shoes. Those two things have always been my dreams! Everyone is looking at me. And that wonderful music starts right up again.

So I start to walk down the aisle. Exactly like I practiced. And it is very fun! I throw those petals right down. And it is a wonderful feeling being the only flower girl!

- -

The next part of that wedding is very boring. A lot of talking. And a lot of standing. My legs are hurting, and I am trying not to get too fidgety.

But then we get to have a very big dinner. And lots of cake.

And there is a DJ playing lots of music. So I do not even need to bring my bongo drums in from the car. I am dancing my butt off. So is Kaitlyn. So is Maybelle. Even my mom and dad are dance, dance, dancing the night away.

Cousin Angela does not get to come back to that wedding. I think she is having too much of a very big fit.

I am just getting ready to get another very big piece of cake with strawberries on it when Mr. Tuttle shows up.

"Mr. Tuttle!" I say. "You cannot come to weddings!"

"It is Saturday," Mr. Tuttle says. "The day Maybelle is supposed to be coming back to the castle. I already told you."

"Yes, well, Maybelle is a big mess with her magic, remember?" I do not think Mr. Tuttle has a good memory. Probably because he is a little bit old.

Maybelle gives a big nod. "Yes, I am a horrible mess," she says.

"So far she has already made someone's shoes orange," I tell Mr. Tuttle. "This wedding was ruined because of her. Now excuse me, please, but it is time for me to get some more cake." I am keeping an eye on that cake. Because it looks like it might be running out. That is because Cousin Harold has eaten four whole pieces. That is called taking more than your share.

"Wait a minute, please, Hailey," Mr. Tuttle says. He is looking down at his clipboard. "Maybelle can stay here."

"Yay!" I say.

"Yay!" Maybelle says.

"But she is going to need some help with her magic," Mr. Tuttle says.

"I will help her. I am very good at helping. One time I even got student of the month for most helpful." That is not exactly true. But it is true that I should have gotten it. I would probably be in second place. And that does count. Second place is a good place to be.

"She needs more help than you can give her," Mr. Tuttle says.

"No, I don't," Maybelle says. "Hailey can help me."

"No," Mr. Tuttle says. "You need another sprite to help you."

"Another sprite?" I ask him. I am getting a very weird feeling in my stomach. A very scared and nervous one.

And then, all of a sudden, there is another sprite here! She is small and has sparkly green wings and long brown hair.

"Hello," she says. "I am Poppy."

"Two sprites?" I ask. I am not sure exactly how I am going to be able to handle this...

Acknowledgments

Thanks to all the usual suspects—Alyssa Henkin, Rebecca Fraser, Aubrey Poole, Kristin Zelazko, Dominique Raccah, Kelly Barrales-Saylor, and everyone else at Sourcebooks for being so amazing.

About the Author

Lauren Barnholdt loves reading, writing, and anything pink and sparkly. She's never had a magic sprite, but she does have four guinea pigs. She lives outside Boston with her husband. Visit her website and say hello at www.laurenbarnholdt.com.

About the Illustrator

Suzanne Beaky grew up in Gahanna, Ohio, and studied illustration at Columbus College of Art and Design. Her expressive illustrations are commissioned by children's book, magazine, and educational publishers worldwide. She and her husband live in Huntingdon, Pennsylvania, with their cats who insist on sitting in her lap while she works and often step in her paint.

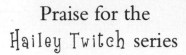

Praise for the
Hailey Twitch series

"The cantankerous Mr. Frisk doesn't stand a chance against precocious Hailey Twitch and her impish fairy Maybelle...Hailey's child-centered perceptions remain spot-on, combining laugh-out-loud moments with gentle insight...This winning series depicts one youngster's balancing act between her sweet and spunky sides and provides a welcome resource for kids waiting for the next Clementine or Moxy Maxwell." —*Kirkus*

"I seemed to be either grinning or laughing aloud as I read the book."
—*The Book Chook*

"With its short chapters, short, choppy sentences, and adorable drawings by artist Suzanne Beaky, *Hailey Twitch is Not a Snitch* is perfect for the emerging reader."
—*Young Adult (& Kids!) Book Central*

"A great chapter book for kids."   —*Reading, Writing, and Waiting*

"If I was still in the classroom, with kinder or first- or second-grade students, this would be my new chapter book series of choice to introduce them to. It is funny, realistic, and teaches a lesson."
—*Write for a Reader*

"An adorable read."   —*The Neverending Shelf*